SOPHIE
SLEEPS OVER

MARISABINA RUSSO

A NEAL PORTER BOOK
ROARING BROOK PRESS
NEW YORK

For Jane, Judy, and Suzannah

Copyright © 2014 by Marisabina Russo
A Neal Porter Book
Published by Roaring Brook Press
Roaring Brook Press is a division of Holtzbrinck Publishing Holdings Limited Partnership
175 Fifth Avenue, New York, New York 10010
The artwork for this book was created using gouache paint.
mackids.com

Library of Congress Cataloging-in-Publication Data
Russo, Marisabina, author, illustrator.
    Sophie sleeps over / Marisabina Russo. — First edition.
        pages cm
    Summary: Sophie is nervous and excited about her first sleepover, but
when she meets her best friend Olive's other best friend, Penelope,
Sophie wants nothing more than to go straight home.
    ISBN 978-1-59643-933-7 (hardcover)
    [1. Sleepovers—Fiction. 2. Best friends—Fiction. 3.
Friendship—Fiction. 4. Rabbits—Fiction.] I. Title.
    PZ7.R9192Sop 2014
    [E]—dc23

                                                          2013011277

Roaring Brook Press books may be purchased for business or promotional use. For information on bulk purchases
please contact Macmillan Corporate and Premium Sales Department at
(800) 221-7945 x5442 or by email at specialmarkets@macmillan.com.

First edition 2014
Book design by Jennifer Browne
Printed in China by Toppan Leefung Printing Ltd., Dongguan City, Guangdong Province

1 3 5 7 9 10 8 6 4 2

From the first day of kindergarten
Sophie and Olive were best bunny friends.

They both snacked on
carrots and cabbage and kale.

They both wore tiaras
and bracelets and bows.

They both played jump rope
and hopscotch and tag.

And, of course, they both loved Ping-Pong.

One day as Sophie and Olive were walking home from school, Olive said, "For my birthday I'm going to have a sleepover party and you're invited."

"Sleepover parties are my favorite kind," said Sophie, even though she had never been to one.

Sophie went home and made a list of what she thought
she would need at Olive's sleepover party:

1 Rainbow tee shirt

2 ping pong paddle

3 tiara

Mama suggested pajamas and a toothbrush.

Daddy suggested a sleeping bag and pillow.

"And what about Turnip?" said Mama. Turnip was
Sophie's favorite doll.

Sophie shook her head. She always slept with Turnip,
but she didn't want Olive to think she was a baby.

The day of Olive's sleepover party, Sophie stuffed everything she needed into a big pillowcase, except for her tiara, which she wore on her head. She carried a box wrapped in purple tissue paper, Olive's favorite color. *My first sleepover party!* thought Sophie. She was happy from the tops of her ears to the tips of her toes.

But when the door opened at Olive's house, instead of Olive, there was a bunny Sophie had never seen before. "Who are you?" asked the bunny.

For a moment Sophie thought maybe she had gone to the wrong house.

"My name is Sophie. Who are you?"

"I'm Penelope," said the bunny. "I'm Olive's best friend."

"No, I'm her best friend," said Sophie, but all of a sudden she wasn't so sure.

First, the three bunnies played Ping-Pong.
Even though Sophie loved to play
Ping-Pong, she kept missing
the ball, and then
she tripped

and her tiara went flying.

"I guess I'm not very good at Ping-Pong today,"
said Sophie, brushing off her skirt.

"Are you good at math?" asked Penelope. "You could just keep score."
Sophie wasn't very good at math, and she didn't want to keep
score. She wanted to go home.

After Ping-Pong, it was time to decorate cupcakes. There were sprinkles and candies and little tubes of frosting.

"I love cupcakes," said Penelope. "Carrot is my favorite."

"Mine, too," said Olive.

"Actually, I kind of like broccoli cupcakes," said Sophie.

"Yuck!" said Penelope and Olive at the same time.

Sophie looked at the clock. Maybe it wasn't too late to call Mama.

But when Olive said, "It's time to play Pin the Tail on the Raccoon!" Sophie decided she could call Mama later.

Olive went first because it was her birthday. Her tail ended up by the raccoon's nose. Penelope went next and her tail ended up by the raccoon's front paw. Finally, it was Sophie's turn. She put the tail right where it belonged.

"You're the winner!" said Olive.

"Were you peeking?" asked Penelope.

"That's cheating," said Olive. "And Sophie would never cheat."

See, I really am Olive's best friend, thought Sophie.

Now she didn't want to go home at all.

When Olive started to open her presents, Penelope shouted, "Mine first!"

Olive ripped the paper and there was a box of paints. "Thank you, Penelope," she said.

Then Olive opened Sophie's gift. Out of the purple tissue she pulled a wooden frame with a photograph of her and Sophie. On the frame, Sophie had painted flowers and the words *Best Friends*.

"Wait, I thought *I* was your best friend, Olive," said Penelope.

"You are," said Olive. "But so is Sophie."

"That's dumb," said Penelope. "A best friend means one friend not two."

"No, it doesn't," said Olive.

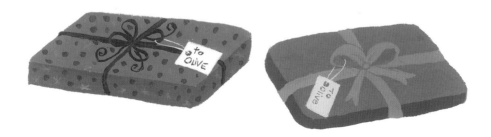

Sophie didn't say anything, but
she kind of agreed with Penelope.

And then it was time for the bunnies to get into their sleeping bags.

"Can we have blueberry pancakes for breakfast?" asked Olive when her mother came in to turn out the lights.

"Of course," said Olive's mother. "Now sleep tight little bunnies, and don't stay up all night."

Soon Sophie could hear soft snoring. The clock on the wall ticked and tocked. She looked around the room. The shadows were all wrong.

She rolled this way and that. She felt scrunched in her sleeping bag and worst of all, she missed Turnip.

Sophie got up and walked to the window.

Suddenly a voice said, "What are you doing?"

Sophie jumped, but it was only Penelope standing right beside her.

"I can't sleep," whispered Sophie.

"Me neither," said Penelope.

"This is my first sleepover," said Sophie.

"Mine, too," said Penelope.

"And I didn't bring my favorite doll to sleep with," said Sophie.

"Me neither," said Penelope. "I didn't want Olive to think I was a baby."

The two bunnies stood by the window
and looked at the shadows of the trees.

They listened to the hoot-hoot of an owl. Penelope showed
Sophie the Big Dipper and the Little Dipper in the starry night
sky. Penelope knew all about the stars.

At last, Sophie yawned and said, "I'm getting sleepy."

Penelope yawned and said, "Me, too."

They both got back in their sleeping bags.

"Maybe Olive's right," whispered Penelope. "Maybe it's okay to have two best friends."

"I guess you can never have too many," said Sophie.

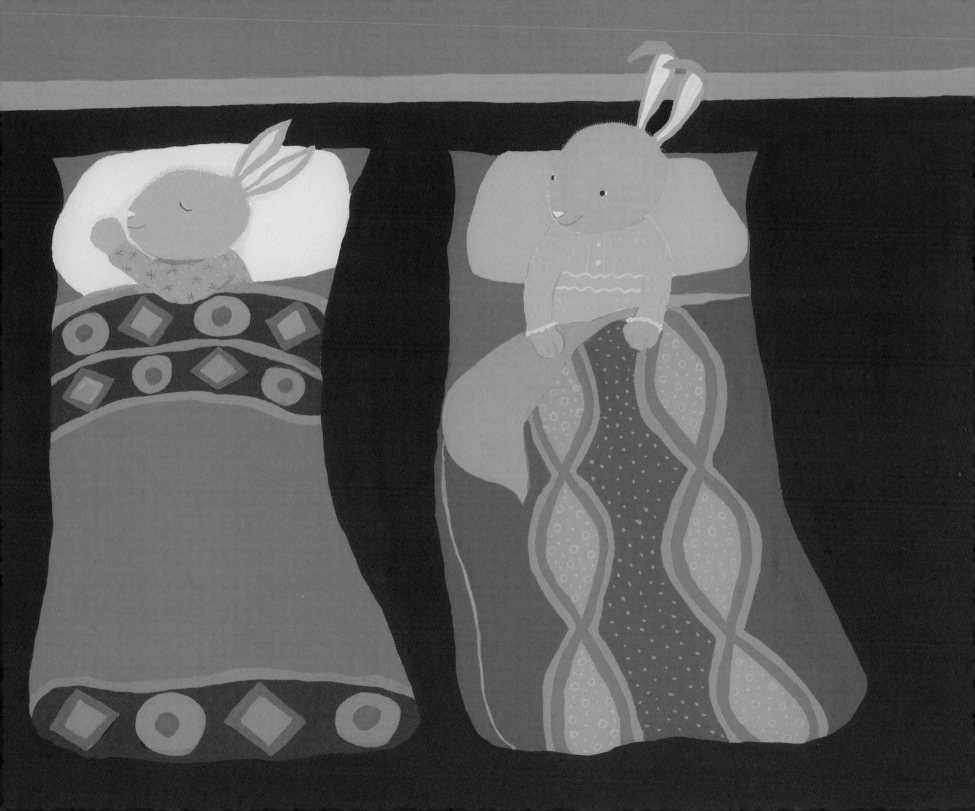

They both listened to Olive snoring. The clock on the wall ticked and tocked. Tomorrow morning there would be blueberry pancakes and Ping-Pong and maybe even time for some jump rope. Jump rope was always better with three.

Sophie was happy from the tops of her ears to the tips of her toes.

And before long she was fast asleep.